D1003243

Kim;
The Story of John

BY
GEE JOYNER

authorHOUSE®

AuthorHouse™
1663 Liberty Drive, Suite 200
Bloomington, IN 47403
www.authorhouse.com
Phone: 1-800-839-8640

First published by AuthorHouse 3/12/2008

ISBN: 978-1-4343-4825-8 (sc)

Printed in the United States of America
Bloomington, Indiana

This book is printed on acid-free paper.

Contents

BLACK GI
GOT TAIL

FOREWORD

The following letters were discovered tucked away in the attic of my home. To protect the identity of the author and recipient of these letters, anonymity is exhibited throughout the text of the letters themselves. By all means, the accounts that are within the body of these letters are true. Given permission from the recipient of these letters, I have structured the correspondence in a format that would be suitable and comprehendible for a public audience and forum. As a complete work or text, the letters are pertinent to the entire American population, not only because of their historical content, but the social commentary that lies within and between the lines of each and every letter written as a necessary footnote to United States history and the warfare that has aided in substantiating the nation as the "Superpower" that the International media has crowned her. Without further ado, I present to the open eye, **Black GI Got Tail**.

Dear Homeboy,

Would you ever believe that I would be a diet specialist? Me neither. They give you a lot of code numbers for the jobs that are offered. I'm also being trained and certified as a corpsman, which is a better name for a glorified nurse's aid. No, there's no sugar in my tank, it's just that there ain't no woman here, so the hard legs gotta do the chick jobs too. I can't say whether I like Virginia or not. All we've been doing is training, eating, and sleeping. Considering Daddy worked the shit outta us when we were kids, I'm sort of fond of this shit. Most of these white boys complain about the work and the order taking, but that's good in my eyes. Hell, niggas been living like this from the get-go. I ain't had a chance to go into town yet.

A few soul brothers and redneck white boys caught a ride into Petersburg last Saturday, but I missed it. I ended up learning how to play chess with a nigga from D.C. named Tony Nelson. Nelson reminds me a lot of you. Wild, uncouth, and about as honest as a slave at a lynching. But that's what I like about him. We talked all night about our hometowns and high schools. Man, you wouldn't believe how much we got in common. He's got a little baby and gal at home and don't know whether or not he's gonna marry the gal. That storyline sounds familiar, don't it? I gave him some good advice though. I told him we got all the time in the world. No need to rush into anything. Nelson's gonna be all right. He seems to be a down nigga and you know I know my down ass niggas. One thing I can say is that he sends an allotment back to his gal and baby and that's more than what a lot of these guys with legit families do. Most of these dudes drink up all their money. Even the white boys fuck off their checks. But I know most of them probably got momma and daddy covering they asses, so they cool.

Nobody is really saying much about the shit over in Vietnam. But we been told that more U.S. advisors have been getting killed over there. Momma told me to stay up on the papers because white folks read the paper and they know what's really goin' on out here. So I've been reading the paper and Time magazine. The white boy who bunks

5

with me, Matt, gets them sent from home. You know what? Momma was right. Them white folks read so much to stay up on politics and shit. All these articles in the paper and Time keep talking about how LBJ is sending more and more GIs over there. But, I doubt I get stationed over there. But if I do, it's cool. I heard them broads got sideways pussies.

Yours truly,

Airman 3rd class
AF148017019

July 17, 1966   *Whiteman's Air Force Base*
                                                              Knobnoster, Missouri

Dear Homeboy,

      Well, I'm at my new "Home Sweet Home." My permanent duty station. We are sixty miles south of Kansas City. Boy does the name fit. Whiteman's? There are no black folk here outside of the ones in the service. I can't wait to see everybody. We're supposed to be here for two or three years. Well, everybody that got here with me at least. Luckily, Nelson got put here with me. We decided to room together since he and I already know each other. How's everyone? Momma said she saw you at church and you looked "good enough to eat." How good is that anyway? I wish I could get to church like I used to. I just don't get off listening to these honkey preachers. They so boring. The music ain't worth what the little bird left on the tree. And the singing is way too tame for me. I like some whoopin' and hollerin'. Some shouting and some jumping around like a jackrabbit on fire. I want to feel like the preacher been through as rough a time as I have all week. These white folks praise God like he's just a friend of theirs they visiting on Sunday for a little while. Hell, the service is too damned short for me. Twenty minutes and we gone. That ain't enough time for God. Momma told me that and she's right.

      I've been telling Nelson about you and he said he's gonna induct you into his 'down ass nigga club.' I told him how we used to be as close as wolves of the same pride back home. How we used to kick a motherfucker's ass if he looked like he wanted some. How you'd pounce on a nigga who wanted to pounce on me before I even had an opportunity to recognize the pounce. I told him about Mr. Alfred's hamburgers. Do you know this nigga wants my sister to send him one in the mail? I told that clown that the post office don't mail meat, but he don't give a damn. He still wants one. Hell, I could use one myself. The food on base is cool, but it's nothing I would write home about. The officers eat good though. They have T-bone steaks and mashed potatoes and gravy as thick as your mama's thighs. And salad with big chunks of tomatoes as big as your balls. Shit, they eat good. Hell, I'm writing home about it.

      But enough complaining. I'm getting the chance to go to school while I'm here. For free. Travel for free. And get paid to do it.

Maybe this white man's service ain't that bad. Two or three years here is enough time for me to get a degree. Then I can come home, get a job, hire you, and be your boss. Well, I gotta go. Nelson just walked through the door holding his fist. He does this shit every night before lights out. He claims this is his prayer to the 'Black God.' He holds up his fist and says,

Now I lay my black ass down to sleep
I pray the Lord my soul to keep
And if my black ass dies before I wake
I pray the Lord is black.'

Ain't this nigga foolish? Nelson sends his regards. Stay cool. Tell your folks I asked about them and that I am cool as usual. I'll catch up with you later.

Yours Truly,

Airman 3rd class
AF148017019

October 10, 1966   *Whiteman's Air Force Base*
                                                      Knobnoster, Missouri

Dear Homeboy,

   What's happening on your side? All is well here. School is
going great. Everything is copasetic. How do you like that big word
I dropped on you? The truth is that copasetic is actually not a real
word. Bill 'Bojangles' Robinson coined that word. Just a tid-bit of
knowledge I think you should know. See, niggas have even invented
words that white folks use. Ain't that some shit. I guess we can do
more than just entertain. Of course, Bojangles Robinson did make
his living tap dancing for white folks. One outta two ain't bad. So,
who knows? Anyway, life on the base is the usual. Wake up at 3a.m.
Work. Eat. Work. Eat. Unwind for all of an hour. Study. Lights
out at 11. Unless you do like I do. Some nights I sneak out and keep
the guys pulling guard duty company. I let them quiz me on the shit
I gotta know for school. It helps. You wouldn't believe how much
information you can retain when a motherfucker is quizzing you by
flashlight. Momma was right. "You learn more in a thicket than you
do on a bed of roses." Plus, if the Sergeant was to catch me, I'd be
pulling KP for a month of Sundays. And God knows pouring peas for
5,000 hungry GI's ain't my style.
   Dig this. KP lasts from 3 a.m. to midnight. You gotta feed
mouths and clean up as you go. And you don't wanna know about
mopping the mess hall. They want this bitch as clean as a nun's pussy.
Not a spot better be on the tables or the floor. Imagine this. Mounds
of peas, chicken fried steak, steak-fried steak, yo' momma fried steak,
and fried chicken skin with the occasional piece of jello caked on top.
Shall I go on? I won't. I'm glad to hear the job at Firestone is going
well. A gig paying $125 a week cutting rubber for tires ain't bad.
Now you can pay me back for sending you all these thimbles from
everywhere I go. I even got some of the cats here getting their folks
to send thimbles from where their from so your collection won't be so
piss-poor. But, I sure am proud of you. We both seem to be heading
in the right direction. Be cool, nigga.
   P.S. Tell your daddy I don't believe he knows Raymond C.
Firestone. You got that job on your own!

February 25, 1967   *Whiteman's Air Force Base*
                                              Knobnoster, Missouri

Dear Homeboy,

I made Sergeant, nigga. So, now I'm gonna really boss your ass around when I see you. Nineteen years old ain't half bad for making Sergeant. My superior officers are proud as hell and you oughta see the look on the faces of everybody. But they lucky I'm a down ass nigga. They've finally been giving me some respect, not much, but some, since I had to kick one of their asses on GP.

A short, stocky, nigga named Rebus been disrespecting my stripes from jump street but I haven't let it get to me until as of late. He thinks because he's from Philly that he's a gangster, but he ain't shit. He is as black as oil and as muscular as Jim Brown and Johnny Sample put together. The soul brothers and white boys fear this nigga like he's God. But I don't. Anyway, he confronted me the other day in the mess hall and told me I only made Sergeant because it's wartime and niggas make rank quick because of motherfuckers dyin' and shit. I told him he was full of shit. Then he had the audacity to grin like a Cheshire cat as he knocked his carton of milk and the food on his tray onto my shoes. Everyone was served their food, yet he was permitted to pour his own poison because KP was scared of him too. But you know me. I remained professional. I'm a non-commissioned officer now.

The soul brothers and the white boys got a laugh on my behalf, but I remained calm. Later on that night, I conned two Mexicans into tying Rebus to his bed. That nigga sleeps hard and don't nothing come to a sleeper but dreams. So, I paid his roommate ten dollars to leave and promised him I'd accidentally forget his head count the next day in order for him to count a few extra sheep. (Black sheep I hope) Of course you know I kept the lights out and beat his ass with a flashlight until he was as silly as a one-legged clown on stilts. Then I flipped the lights on and went back to my room. All of the other cats either heard him screaming like a castrated mule and saw me leaving or heard about it from his roommate. You know, sometimes the legend is greater than the man. They all think I'm a crazy, little nigga now. But I like it that way. Now they'll respect me. Just like I respect you, Mr. Firestone. Stay cool.

Airman 2ⁿᵈ Class
AF148017019

Dear Homeboy,

They're sending me to Phang Rang. It's in Vietnam, nigga. I don't know what to expect. I never thought I'd be sent over there. They told me I was gonna be stationed in Thailand. Then the next thing I know, headquarters sends for me and my balls to get busted. Everybody seems to be excited for me because I'm gonna probably get the chance to see some action and I guess that's cool. I'll get the opportunity to follow in daddy's footsteps. He and I are gonna be the only members of the family who have fought in a war. He tells me WWII was worse than eating a porcupine's pussy. He said Germany was 'Hell in a handbasket!' Momma says he' never been to Germany, let alone fight there. You know Daddy, though, he exaggerates. He's full of tall tales. He'd say he captured Hitler but let him go if he can keep your attention. 'Hell in a handbasket.' I wonder what that shit means anyway? Who knows? I hope Vietnam ain't like that. It looks like we gonna go in and light up some Chinks and get back home. No sweat. If I can survive growing up in our neighborhood, I can survive anywhere.

They're sending me to San Francisco for a jungle-training refresher course. I'm supposed to be there for six goddamn weeks. I hope we don't run into those "hippies" or whatever the hell they call themselves out there. They're gonna fuck around and get their asses kicked. I'll probably make their funky asses take a bath afterwards. Nelson already left a couple of weeks ago, so I think he's gonna give me a refresher course of his own. That nigga loves the clubs. He uses the stripes to get pussy. That shit works too! Plus, he draws on a fake goatee cause he says it "makes a nigga look more dignified." He better hope he don't ever get a hold of some permanent ink. Shit, the officers will have his ass. And you know how white folks love coon pie.

Before I forget, how in the world are you getting married? You must got a baby on the way or somethin'? You didn't tell me about this in your last letter. I had to find out from my gossipin' ass momma. She said your momma was down at Leo Rosenblum's delicatessen buying up all the cold cuts and shit. Her fat ass!! She told momma everything.

Momma told me. Now, I'm telling you-DON'T DO IT, NIGGA!! Wait till I can get back. I wouldn't want to miss it if my life depended on it. Stay cool, nigga.

Your man,

Buck Sergeant E-4
AF148017019

P.S. Since when did ya'll start eating corn beef?

Dear Homeboy,

This motherfucker is huge. This sprawling, monstrosity will eat our town for breakfast. They got about three hospitals here. It's easy as hell to get lost or not see a motherfucker you know for days at a time. I jawed with Nelson last week and we went into town. No hippies or fags. I guess they know niggas in the service ain't looking to have no booty babies.

Nelson left yesterday, so I haven't really had a chance to enjoy myself. I went with Nelson to the embarkation point at the airport to see him off. That lucky nigga's going to Thailand. There must have been 707s for miles. They had them lined up like cordwood. One hundred sixty-five men getting on and one hundred sixty-five men getting off. Seven days a week, twenty-four hours a day, until the war is over. That's what Nelson said. He wasn't that talkative, but I guess that's because the shit is really sinking in. Everybody was kinda quiet to tell you the truth. They say the flight is twenty hours long. Both to and fro. Funny thing is, some of them won't be having a fro. But I'm not worried about Nelson. He's going to Thailand. He probably won't set foot in Vietnam.

The other cats here seem cool. But we been humping our asses so hard that you don't really get a chance to know anybody. When we get finished for the day, motherfuckers be sleeping like babies. They got me rooming with a white boy. This cat don't ever sleep. He stays up all night doing sit-ups and talking about how he got land waiting for him in Indiana. South Bend, or Evansville, I think? He's got a wife, a kid, a minister for a daddy, and a lush for a momma. Ain't that a dickhead? Hell, my daddy drinks and my momma lives at church. Now that's some irony for your ass. But I like Holder. He's cool for a white boy. Plus, he's clean. I told momma all white folks ain't dirty, but she didn't believe me. She said she'd cleaned enough of their houses to know better.

I'll be getting my MAC boarding pass in a few days or so. So, it's official. Vietnam here I come. No turning back now. I'll be leaving in two weeks, so don't expect to hear from me until I get settled over there. Momma told me to keep the Lord with me. She's so worried about me. But tell her I'm gonna be alright. I think a second opinion will help her out tremendously. Stay cool, nigga.

Your man,

Buck Sergeant E-4
AF148017019

Dear Homeboy,

     I see why they made us send our winter clothes home. It's hotter than two rats fucking in a wool sock over here. We stopped in Anchorage before we left the states and it's funny how you can go from one extreme to another in the matter of a day. One day it's cold, dry, and coarse. The next day, a suffocating torridness becomes your unseen commanding officer. Or should I say the same day? That International Dateline is a son-of-a-bitch. So, actually, I left one day and arrived the same day.

     We landed at Tansanknut to find a troop of slant-eyed motherfuckers who looked as poor as Job's turkey. They're as dark as niggas to me. Hell, just as broke too. So who knows? Maybe I'll have more in common with them than I expect. Anyway, I get transported to Phang Rang, a province of Vietnam, after a couple of more days here. So, it looks like I'll have to nut up to the responsibilities of a Sergeant now. All bets are off. It's wartime now. I'ma have to win one for the home team. I got word that Nelson was in the TAC (Tactical Air Command) and was assigned to maintenance. That nigga is going to be working like a slave in summer. I don't really know what to expect from my assignment. Although I'm SAC (Strategic Air Command), I will be working with the medics. Shit, a nigga don't know nothing about medicine, nursing, doctoring, or any of that shit. But, now is the best time to learn. Momma can't believe it. A male, nigga nurse. Hell, we coming a long way, huh?

     I'm not mad that you went and got hitched without me. But love is an urgent matter. Especially when a child is pending. Shit man, things are changing. Your last letter was quite brief. Momma told me you were attending *Good God Almighty Thank You For Keeping My Lights on Baptist Church* now. Since when did you start worshipping with uppity niggas? Hell, only doctors, lawyers, and Indian chiefs go there. But, I guess that promotion you told me about is paying off. You can afford a wife, a baby on the way, and the inflated tithes of a rich, nigga church. But, it's cool man. Whatever lets your little light shine is fine with me.

I gotta tell you about the animals over here. They got elephants lingering in the streets like we got stray dogs in the neighborhood. This is the funniest shit I've ever seen. But they don't bother anybody. The white boys got the locals to show them how to ride. Hell, the white boys ain't scared of the elephants like the niggas are. The soul brothers don't want nothing to do with them. But we the ones supposed to be from Africa? Don't Africa got elephants? That's funny. Snakes are everywhere you look. Plus, with the funk of burning sulfur to stop the bites of mosquitoes, a nigga rarely got time to worry about the Lucifers lurking around. You don't fuck with them. They don't kill your black ass. You dig?

Well, I gotta split. I really don't have a lot of time to be fucking off anymore. We gotta to go on a search and destroy mission in three days and I don't know when I'll get a chance to get at you again. So don't wait up. Once again, congratulations to you and the other half of your soul. I'm glad you found it. I'm gonna have to find mine when I get home.

Your man,

Buck Sergeant E-4
AF148017019

Dear Homeboy,

Fuck you, nigga! I was joking about the bourgeois nigga church. You sensitive all of a sudden? I guess marriage makes you like that. Don't write me with that kinda shit anymore. I ain't the same nigga you think I am. I'm a SAC trained killer now. I get paid to steal lives at the blurt of a command. So, don't test me! Apparently, you haven't been watching the tube over there. Motherfuckers over here are going through Hell. "Hell in a hand basket" like daddy said. Man, niggas getting killed like flies. One day you're raiding a hutch with a cat and the next day he fucks up and steps on a mine. Lucky him, huh? These sneaky ass Vietcong got booby traps everywhere. And there ain't no way you can spot 'em. It's pure luck if you miss one and pure fate if you hit one. All the jungle looks the same. A green blanket.

Working in the medics don't help none either. I'm collecting hands, fingers, feet, toes, noses, dicks, and assholes all day long. I'm not cracked up for this shit. It's funny what you can get used to though. The first time I saw a dead body, I froze like ice water and threw up when I saw the facial expression on the corpse. Fear is a motherfucker. And I don't want no part of it. Man, the look in his eyes and the way his mouth gaped open made me think about what this cat's last thoughts were. Not home, I bet. Survival probably. That's what it's all about now. So, fuck home. Momma's worries and your bitchin' is more than I can handle. I need encouragement and courage. Home-cooking if you got it. Something I can feel and taste. Write me about good things from now on. Worry about me and not so much about yourself. You're cool right now. I'm the one fighting for life every day. No, not every day. Because the days we're not in the field, we're waiting to be called. Ain't that a bitch? Death even calls on your off days. Anyway, can't wait to get back to the world.

Buck Sergeant E-4

Dear Homeboy,

I haven't heard from you since my last letter home. What, Firestone don't teach its nigga foremen how to write? Damn, don't forget a nigga. I'm hanging in there, though. Momma said your daddy has been low sick and that you've been taking it hard. Stay cool. You'll get through it. Hell, you pay your preacher enough! But, I hope everything pans out.

They got us living in these cramped hooches with four or six motherfuckers in each one. Either way, it's too many motherfuckers for me. A man needs to be alone sometimes and you rarely get that chance over here. I'm beginning to feel caged in. I don't know what the next day holds and I feel a sense of urgency for me to do something, but I don't know what. All I smell every day is garlic. Seems like the Vietnamese bathe in the shit. They use it in all the food. A lot of the mess hall workers are Vietnamese or Thai girls. Some of them are fine too. The white boys call them goat smellers, garlic heads, and gooks. Now that's a dickhead. We're in their country. I guess the white man don't give a damn though. Hell, the U.S. is building roads and bridges and providing employment to them, so I guess the white boys got the right to degrade their asses.

There was a monsoon last week, so there was rain for days. The Clung overflowed and flooded a small area of the base. Now, the Clung is full of the area's piss, shit, dead animals, food, and every other thing you can think of. Shit, the base was funky as a billy goat's gruff. It was like an obstacle course trying to walk around the pissy pools of terds. But somehow we managed. Well, I don't want to bore you with my tales of Nam, so I won't. But I will tell you one thing. Guns wield power. For some reason, I feel like I'm in control when I'm behind that M60. You know, when I'm gunning randomly into the air, murdering oxygen and unknown Vietcong soldiers, I feel at that particular moment that I have control over whether I live or die. Not the Vietcong. Not God. But me. Now whether I slip up or not is on me. In war, no mistakes are allowed.

Your man,

Buck Sergeant
AF148017019

January 14, 1968   *Phang Rang Air Force Base*
                                      Phang Rang, Vietnam

Dear Homeboy,

So, you think I'm a killer now? Motherfucker, I'm a soldier. I have no choice. It's easy for you to say. Mr. Firestone won't kill you if you half-ass do your job. If I slack off at work, I die. I told you I don't need this type of shit from home. No encouragement? Damn you then. Maybe you shouldn't write me anymore. Everybody is on a nigga's ass. Hell, these white boys have even told the whores that the niggas are monkeys. So, the Vietnamese whores say, "Black GI got tail" when some of the soul brothers proposition them for some tutu. It's cool though. Whenever I hear them say that shit, I tell them, "Buddha got tail." Shit, they cry like babies and say, "He speak number ten on Buddha." Number ten is bad. But they'll give niggas some tutu when the white boys ain't around. It' funny, but the white boys got their own separate group of Vietnamese whores they patronize and the niggas got their own whores. Now, the ones who fuck the peckerwoods don't fuck the niggas and the ones who fuck the niggas, well of course they fuck the honkeys too. It's funny how the Air Force allows prostitution on the base. But I guess if you wanna keep tension down and morale up, you've gotta pacify the hard-ons. Pussy calms the savage beast, you know.

Man, I don't know whether I'm coming or going anymore. They got us killing the Vietcong, yet we're feeding them too. How you gonna ransack a village then drop rice on it? And to think, we're supposed to be over here participating in a 'humanitarian' effort. Ain't no humanity in this. Ho Chi Min got niggas over here fighting for South Vietnam and don't even know it, or probably doesn't give a fuck. The Russians are backing North Vietnam, so a nigga can kill a peckerwood for free. No time served, no wrung neck, no nothing. Well, I gotta go. More killing to do. Just bullshitting. We don't kill every day, nigga.

Buck Sergeant E-4
AF148014019

P.S. Just every other day!!!

19

Dear Homeboy,

Be cool over there. I haven't heard from you in a while, but I understand. All Hell done broken loose on base. The last week has been a war within a war. Niggas knockin' white boys out left and right. I got word of Dr. King's murder when Holder and me were coming back from Papa San's market. When we got back, I saw cats laid out like slaughtered hogs. I thought the Vietcong had attacked us. Me and Holder were running to the barracks when a nigga named Black Tom told us Dr. King had been shot dead in Memphis. I couldn't believe it. Man, the first thing I did was run into the first honkey I saw. The messed up thing about that is that it was Holder.

I don't know why I did it. I mean, I know why, but I had no reasoning behind it. Holder is a motherfucker I live with. A motherfucker I eat with and fight with. He is a fellow GI. But, he's white. I guess I did it cause he's white. He didn't do shit either. He just clutched the mouse over his eye like a stolen purse and walked back to the barracks. Niggas fought all night long. Jumping on white boys like trampolines. Air police earned their keep that night. Now, everyone keeps to themselves. Blacks with the blacks and the whites with the whites. It's better this way. Now we know where we stand.

We're fighting for them over here, but they don't give a fuck. Ray Earl Ray or whatever the fuck the asshole's name is who shot Dr. King killed the only nigga that could talk to them white folks in Washington. Niggas been crying and shit, wondering how we gonna get a fair shake from Whitey now that King is dead. I don't blame ya'll for rioting over there. We're right with you. Fuck all that integration shit. White folks don't wanna be fair, so why should we? Separate but equal. That's some real shit. Why not? It's cool.

Hell, white folks got the gooks hating niggas, they already hate niggas, and some niggas even hate niggas. You know, some black cats over here got the nerve to say that King was a troublemaker and that we need to quit complaining because "niggas done come a long way."(I gotta let you know these are the words of Uncle Toms and not me) Man, between the deaths and the niggas on dope(Robitussin, weed, heroin, cocaine, opium), I don't know if I can maintain. There's no sobriety here. We all are getting high off of something. A nigga needs something over here. Some niggas lush up, splurge on pussy, dope up, or re-enlist for multiple TDYs(Tour of Duties). And some niggas get high on home, not knowing there might not be a home to go back to. Things change a lot in twenty-six months!

I know things have changed for me. You and I are experiencing things that we didn't know we would. We're growing up. Stability is your cot, while I slumber on a pallet of ifs, ands, maybes, and mights. You're living, my man. Me? I'm attempting to live. Lost in a world of bullets, protocols, and manifested tactical trainings. I can't keep wondering, nigga. But I can keep wandering. The more I think of you and the world, the more I become a stranger to what I thought home was. I know it ain't here, but I know it ain't there either.

Word has it that Nelson's daddy died and he had to fly back to the States. Some of the GIs who visited Tahkli where Nelson was stationed said Nelson went AWOL on the visit back to the World. I guess he couldn't deal with the loss of his daddy. Damn, that was my man. I didn't think he could do no shit like that, but only that particular person knows his wills and won'ts and do's and don'ts. You really don't know a person after you get to the war. You just never really know. Holder and I have patched things up. I let him get a free one off of me for the shiner I gave him. Now we both look like one-eyed 'coons. Take care of yourself and I'll try to do the same.

Buck Sergeant E-4
AF148017019

P.S. I pray the war will be over soon. Don't wait for me and definitely don't count the days. I'll catch up with you…hopefully.

AFTERWORD

Two months after the receipt of the last letter, the recipient was paid a visit from the United States Air Force. The nature of the visit was to inform the recipient that the sender of the letters, after several weeks of an attempted search and rescue mission, was declared Missing in Action. Though the military had no knowledge of the soldier's whereabouts or physical condition, they did not believe him to be deceased. Therefore, the U.S. Air Force stated that they would continue searching for the soldier who was lost in combat. After a three-hour interview with the recipient of the letters, I was informed that the person they knew prior to the war, in their mind, was "lost" long before that fateful visit from Air Force representatives.

Kim;
The Story of
John

Part 1

"How you gon' have more hair in your booty hole than you got around your dick, Caaaapp?" Embarrassed, the 22-year-old looked shyly away from Kim as she openly ridiculed what she considered to be Capp's lackluster, if not peculiar, anatomical attributes. Both Kim and Capp were lying on the bed. Capp was bottomless, but Kim remained fully clothed. Bored and slightly humiliated by Kim's under-the-table remark, Capp popped up off of the bed like a pop tart from a toaster and began dressing. He exited the bedroom and went into the living room of the hacienda that he shared with his roommate Tawson, with whom he had been friends with since the summer before their freshman year in college. He fumbled on the coffee table looking for his lighter, found it, then went into the kitchen and got a knife and scissors from the drawer next to the refrigerator.

"Caaaaap? "

"Cool out, Kim. I'ma be back in there in a lil' bit. Why don't you call your girl Patrice? My man Tawson's gon' be home from work in a few. Maybe you can get her over here and you, me, her, and him can set it off in this bitch, you hear me?!"

"Alright," Kim replied with a lustful whisper. "I'm fixin' to give her a call now." While talking, Kim came into the living room area, sat down, and began flipping through the Playboy magazines that Capp had subscribed to and convinced his roommate to display on the coffee table as to be an ever-present aphrodisiac for female company.

"Capp, look at these white girls' booties. They flat as pancakes."

From the kitchen, Capp began to snicker. "With no syrup… But I'd still fuck 'em though."

"Whatcha doin' in there anyway, Caaaaapp?"

"I'm do-in what I want I feel like doin', Kim. And quit sing-songin' my name like that. I don't like that type of shit." The tone in Capp's voice suddenly crescendoed from sarcastic to cold and honest.

"You mean, Capp. You a mean motherfuckerrrr." Kim allowed the "r" to roll off her tongue and skip like a broken record.

"I'm about to smoke. You smoke?"

"Smoke what?"

"Weed."

"Oh, no. I thought you were talking about cigarettes."

" Naw, I don't fuck with them cowboy killers." Capp walked into the living room with marijuana- filled cigars behind his left and right ears and one dangling like a participle from the right corner of his mouth.

"That is *not* sexy," Kim sassed.

"Ain't tryin' to be," Capp countered.

Though all of the lights were out, the hacienda was illuminated by the numerous candles that Capp routinely lit and strategically placed around the bachelor pad when in expectance of female company, which he and his roommate would call "games." The bachelors would dialogue about the women they wished to have sexual relations with as if the women were their opponents and each individual man was a sports franchise in and of itself. Capp and Tawson spoke of their female companions and conquests as past, future, or present "basketball games." Each man would liken himself to either a past or present NBA player and speak of his level of intimacy with a particular young woman in terms of statistical information. For instance, the meeting, greeting, and exchanging of telephone numbers was the "tip off" to a game, and the more intimate, either mentally or physically, one got with a woman, the more "points" they scored or "turnovers" they induced. Now, if one of them changed a female's mind from not wanting to sleep with them to allowing them to have sexual intercourse, that was considered a turnover by the woman and a "steal" for the men. If they had their sights set on the a woman who was already involved with another man, then the guys would be competing against the other man rather than the woman, and if they happened to bed the female in the process of trying to make her choose him over her current resident lover, then this was also considered a "steal."

Capp pulled his Zippo lighter from under the cushion of the couch, a regular hiding place from Tawson and the smoking visitors of their abode who may have found the metallic lighter with a cannabis leaf on the front and a picture of Reggae legend Bob Marley to their liking, and lit the end of his reefer-filled cigar.

"You smoking on that blunt like a dick, ain't it?" Kim said, her face illustrating a crafty smile.

"Say what?" Kim didn't respond to Capp but began to snicker.

"Say what?" Capp repeated. "Bitch, don't play with me like that. Ain't no fag or bitch in me, you hear me?" Kim's face was paralyzed with confusion and disgust.

"Damn," Kim said with a sigh, "I was just playin', shit. You so fuckin' mean!"

The doorknob began to rattle and both Kim and Capp looked towards the hacienda's entrance as the door opened.

"Oh, we've got company, Capp?" Tawson, a slender, dark complexioned young man with coarse, black, straight hair like a Puerto Rican strolled into the living room with an extremely bright smile on his face considering he had done a laborious, six-hour stint at Memphis' Federal Express distribution headquarters and the clock was positioned at 3:15 in the morning. Capp's demeanor immediately changed. His disgruntled facial positioning transformed into a look of pacification and expectancy.

"What's the bees' wax, man?" Tawson, and most Memphians, pronounced "man" as if it was the hair on a male lion or a popular North American street name.

"You got it." Capp responded.

Kim jealously interrupted the brotherly greeting of the two. "Hello, Tawson," said Kim seducingly lingering on the s in his name.

"Where's Pat-ris?"

"Pa-trice is over her auntie's house."

Tawson laughed and scoffed a bit. "Her auntie's house?"

"Yeah," Capp chimed in, "her Aunt Fred."

Capp and Tawson guffawed loudly and gave each other five while clasping their hands together and falling into one another in a quasi-hug as if Capp's snide remark was so humorous as to impede their ability to stand or maintain their composure. Kim grew increasingly frustrated with the continuous laughter of the two.

"Ya'll laughin' like some little bitches, shit."

"I told you about that bitch shit, now, Kim!" Capp, once again, angrily scolded Kim's vulgar labeling of him a *bitch*.

"Aw now, Capp. You gotta smart lip on that one."

"And a deep throat too!" Kim blurted out. Her remark, which was followed by the running of her tongue across her bottom lip, caused both Capp and Tawson to go into attack mode.

"For real?" Upon Tawson's inquiry, he began inching his right hand closer and closer to his pelvic area. "I'ma have to tell Patrice she needs to hire you as her tutor." Jokingly stated, Tawson once again slapped five with Capp.

"Well, shid," Capp said with a whisper, "What's the beeswax, then?"

"Whatcha' mean?" Kim smiled, then once again glossed her bottom lip with her tongue and eked out a sly smile.

"What I mean?" Capp said inquisitively. "It's damned near five in the mornin', you got two dicks, four balls and a quarter ounce of weed in front of you and you askin, 'What I mean?'" Capp began blowing cheerios with the marijuana smoke that bellowed from his charred lips that had darkened from clown-hair red to a purplish brown since his teen years and the genesis of his mild drug addiction.

"You look sexy with your big ol' lips," Kim said enticingly.

"You think?" Capp responded while getting up from the couch and blowing more smoke directly in the direction of Kim. He started moving closer to Kim until they were nose to nose. Tawson plucked the cigar from Capp's left ear and lit it. The room remained as silent and inactive as a dead woman's womb. Capp took another pull of the cigar, inhaled the potent reefer deep into his lungs, beckoned for Kim's mouth with a couple of slow flickers and "come to me's" with his tongue, leaned in with a slight tilt of the head to the right, and began a ten second oral search for her tonsils.

"Mmm, mmm," Tawson hummed as he began groping his privates with his hand.

Kim dropped from the green, leather loveseat to the floor in a hurry. As if possessed, she began panting heavily while she began kissing Capp's stomach and thighs on the outside of his clothes. Still smoking, yet looking at Tawson excitedly and anxiously, Capp lifted his shirt, allowing Kim to kiss and lick his naked flesh. Abruptly, Kim savagely resumed her oral bathing of Capp's penis with her tongue. Kim bypassed the unbuckling and unzipping of Capp's pants and swiftly pulled down his bottoms.

"Oowee, shit!" Capp exalted while Kim was still French kissing the head of his penis while tightly clutching and stroking his shaft with her awkwardly long, light skinned hands. Up and down with the left hand for a few seconds. Then she'd mimic the same with her right hand. Slowly, Tawson inched towards Kim while simultaneously releasing his penis from its prison.

"Feel this one here, lil' Mama." Tawson whispered.

Hearing this, Kim, still orally resuscitating Capp's genitalia, slyly glanced at Tawson's stiffly erect penis and started to fondle his testicles in the palm of her off hand.

"Gon' taste that there, Gon' taste that." Tawson said growing more and more impatient with Kim's nonchalant seductiveness. Tawson grew weary within seconds from the sight of Capp being immersed in oral intercourse and decided to softly guide Kim's head towards his groin area. Kim looked up and winked her eye, "Oh, okay then. With your fat thang." She began licking his pee hole while juggling his testicles.

"Ooh, lemme taste you." Capp stated while masturbating and eerily looking at Tawson being taken to ecstasy with the flick of a tongue. Intoxicated by the weed and the fellatio-filled atmosphere, Capp bent down on his knees and began squeezing the buttocks of Kim. Moving his hands from her rear end to the front of her pants, Capp frantically began undoing the belt buckle of Kim's pants.

"Hold up now." Kim said while grabbing the hands of Capp.

"Just lemme touch it, Kim. Come on and lemme feel those hairs."

Trying to hinder Capp from molesting her privates and maintain Tawson's blowjob became a daunting task. Steadily undoing Kim's pants and feeling the fluff of her pubic hairs, Kim yanked her head away from Tawson's penis and glared maliciously at Capp, yelling, "No goddamit! Damned! Just be cool with getting' your dick sucked.

31

Fuck!" At that moment, Tawson came profusely. It oozed from the head of his penis and began quickly streaming down his shaft. Seeing this eased the situation and Kim started to savagely lick Capp's entire mid section. She shampooed his pubic hairs with her tongue and continued her oral attack on his testicles while Capp masturbated.

"Go ahead and cum, boy. Go 'head, come on." Kim began nibbling on his penis head and sucking and licking his shaft while Tawson leaned up against the entertainment system, continuingly masturbating and enjoying the voyeurism of it all. Following Tawson's lead, Capp too ejaculated. Craning his neck as far back as it could go, Capp let out a low grunt followed by a "Sssssss!" like a snake. Upon hearing the serpentine sound, Kim swallowed Capp's DNA.

After the two young men had burst like balloons, they looked at each other, half-heartedly embarrassed, and laughed like schoolboys rejoicing over an unfoiled folly. Kim, Capp, and Tawson all began gathering their composure. An awkward silence murdered the room. Several seconds went by yet lingered and rattled like a smoker's cough.

"Shid, I'm hungry." Capp quipped yet made his way towards the kitchen. Tawson, still fiddling with the buckle on his work pants followed suit.

"What we eatin' on?" Tawson said with a minute laugh.

"Blunts."

"Well then." Tawson replied and began singing, *"Roll up another one...trick we ain't finished yet,"* alluding to a popular rap tune by Memphis rap legend Gangsta Blac.

Kim, growing fidgety and restless in the living room, began flipping through the numerous channels on the satellite television while playing with her cellular telephone.

"Um, ya'll...I think I'm fina..." Kim paused. Then she continued while glancing at her cellular telephone like it was the dangling watch of a hypnotist, "Um,...I'm finna go."

"For real." Capp's nonchalance was conspicuously noticeable in his tone, and facial expression.

Tawson lazily slurred between the inhaling and exhaling of the weed, "Make sure..." he coughed, then resumed his oral thought, "you get at your girl. Yeah, make sure you tell Patrice to get with me later on today."

"I'll do that." Kim replied as she was leaving. "I'ma talk to you later today, Caaappp."

"I told you bout that shit." This time Capp was laughing as he was chastising Kim for her child-like pronunciation of his given name. He was always sensitive about his name because of the children in the neighborhood and church, and school, and pretty much anywhere he went. People always queried about the origins of and rationale behind his being given this peculiar *nickname* name. Capp's life became especially difficult when Memphis' slanguage added the word "cap" to the lexicon to refer to the act of performing oral copulation. His peers would often make crude jokes about Capp being an expert in the art of oral copulation, but this didn't seem to offend nor humor their female counterparts. In fact, the perverse references to Capp's name created an unprecedented popularity and enigma around him. Being noticeably more attractive than the average male and having a natural comfortablity in his conversation that lured and seduced women like cheese does a rat to a trap, once having met the infamous Capp, both males and females not only liked the young man, but they even endorsed this likeability and coolness to those who only knew of him by the exhausted references to oral copulation. All in all, Capp didn't mind the quirkiness of his name. Not only did it allow his presence to precede him by the mere name itself being popular, but considering he was always fond of the ladies, it also served as the definitive conversational piece.

For the next two weeks, Capp avoided Kim's constant phone calls to study for the Graduate Records Exam so that he could secure his entrance into a reputable graduate program. He either wanted to work on a graduate degree in Political Science or English in order to use a Master's degree in one of those disciplines to prepare him for the extensive reading and writing that would be required for his ultimate academic goal, an admittance to Law School. Because Capp was from a well-to-do family and used his student loan money to pay his portion of the rent, several months in advance, as well as his financial aid disbursement to buy a few pounds of marijuana to sell, the money he earned from working for his father's construction company was what Capp referred to as his "miscellaneous monies." He would indulge weekly on shopping sprees that always included at least two pair of tennis shoes. Capp believed it mandatory for a man to have as many pairs of shoes possible. His fetish with tennis shoes stemmed from his childhood, when no matter the request, his mother only bought three pair of tennis shoes for him a year. A pair for Christmas, a pair for the family summer vacation, and a fresh pair for the beginning of the school year.

Capp was proud and boastful of his shoe collection, particularly the tennis shoes. He had all colors and types. Cocaine white. Charcoal gray. Smoke gray. Running shoes. Canvas sneakers. Basketball shoes. Slip-ons. Velcro. Nike. New Balance. Reebok. Puma, Adidas, Reebok, Fila, and Polo. Any designer one could think of, Capp had them. He seemed to enjoy everything in excess. His shoe collection parroted his love of the accumulation of *things*. When it came to women, it was no different. The same way he treated his shoes, he'd treat his relationships with women. He'd impatiently obtain them because of their outside appearance, unaware of their comfortability, durability, or quality of the shoe, wear them a few times, and keep them on the shelf as insurance policies, if and when the need for them would arise.

During the time Capp was held up at the hacienda studying for his graduate school entrance exam, Tawson worked hard and "played" harder. Tawson worked for Capp's father during the day, went to classes in the evening, romanced Patrice at night, and worked in the Federal Express hub in the twilight hours. Patrice was just as nymphomaniacal as Kim. Capp couldn't relax while Patrice was visiting Tawson. Because of the amazingly loud and dramatic yelps of passion that Patrice continuously belted out, Capp's studies were routinely interrupted. Some evenings, the lustful loudness would prompt Capp to increase the sound of the television or radio, whichever he was using at the moment, and slither down the hallway until he approached the crease of Tawson's bedroom door and pleasured himself by indulging vicariously in Patrice's pants and moans and screams until he too, just as Tawson and Patrice would repeatedly do until time for Tawson to gear up for his duty in the hub, climaxed. Upon his spewing, Capp would shamefully scamper off to the kitchen like a rodent and clean up with a tear from the roll of Bounty that sat conspicuously on the end of the countertop. (It seemed to always serve as Capp's *thicker, quicker, picker-upper.*)

One particular evening, Capp made his clandestine and fantastical activity known to both Tawson and Patrice. Whereas his imagination always halted at the threshold of Tawson and Patrice's doorway to sexual gratification, this particular evening, Capp eased the door open and immediately morphed into a peeping Tom. Like a voyeur, he loomed and peered at the beast with two backs. Up and down, Tawson pumped hard and swift into Patrice's pelvic area.

"Ooh, ooowee, Tawson. Ooooweee." Tawson, silent and dutiful like a centurion, continued his pumping, all the while staying mute and non-responsive to Patrice's lustful ballad.

"Oooh, Tawson. Tho' that dick baby, tho' that dick. Ooohh, aahhh," Patrice continued to exclaim. Now, in a full-scale assault on his genitalia, Capp unabashedly began broadening the opening in the door until he had enough room to slither through. With the door ajar, Capp eased his way into the room and got down onto his knees and crept towards the bed like a housecat. Inching closer and closer to Tawson and Patrice, he reached his hand towards Patrice's flailing leg that was dangling over the side of the bed. With his hand trembling, Capp withdrew his arm and hesitated. Once again, he extended his quaking hand towards Patrice's leg and began softly stroking her calf. Shocked at the fact that Patrice acted as if Tawson had grown tentacles like an octopus, Capp lost himself in the touch. Hearing Patrice's gasping and groaining induced him to go a step further in his search for satisfaction. Capp was now kissing and licking her shins and knees, gradually running his tongue towards her thigh, all the while oblivious to Tawson's continual penetration.

"Uh, who is this?" Patrice said with a giggle and pant, still trying to stick to her script of verbally praising Tawson's evening glory. Capp now began to pant as well.

"Aww, it ain't nobody." Tawson replied.

Patrice now reached her hand out as if to invite Capp into the bed with she and Tawson.

"What you want me to do?" Capp said quickly, now starting to lick her index and middle fingers.

"Whatever you want to do, boy."

"I'ma show you my *boy*." Capp began shucking his clothes as he got up off his knees and began plunging his tongue in and out of her mouth as he stroked his penis until it stood erect and quivering. Penis in hand, Capp stretched his penis out as long as he could by grabbing it at its base and pushing the skin back to his pelvis until his penis appeared to be abnormally long.

"Mmmm, mmm." Patrice said while Tawson kept pumping and occasionally glancing at Capp.

"Here you go, Patrice. Take this here." She opened up her mouth wide as Capp placed the head of his penis inside her mouth, purposely steering clear of her teeth, and began slapping his penis against her tongue. Amused, Patrice began to snicker and then stuck her tongue out as if a doctor was checking her for strep throat, moaned out, "Aaaahhh!", and then vacuumed Capp's genitalia with her lips, every so often softly nibbling his privates like a squirrel does an acorn.

"Lemme get a lil' cap, Capp." Tawson said while ejecting himself from Patrice's womb. Capp halted the fellatio by pulling his penis from Patrice's lips while she jokingly extended her neck like a giraffe as if wanting more of the dangling carrot-treat she was enjoying prior to Tawson's switch-a-roo notion. After changing positions, several times, and pouncing up and down inside of Patrice, the two young men climaxed. Afterwards, Tawson, Capp, and Patrice giggled like embarrassed school children. They promptly dressed, and exited the bedroom, leaving Patrice to take what Capp referred to as a "hoe bath". (A quick scrub of the vagina and rectum with a warm, soapy rag.)

"Man, I gotta get outta here. I'ma be late for work."

"You gone leave before your company goes?"

"I'm leavin' out right behind him." Patrice yelled from Tawson's bedroom.

"Aight then, supersonic." Capp yelled back.

Patrice sashayed her way into the living room and grabbed her purse from the coffee table.

"You ready, lil' mama?"

"After you, sexy."

"Naw, naw. That's you."

"Noooo, that's you."

"How about the both of you just leave, huh?" Capp said laughingly yet growing frustrated with the phony lovey dovey talk from Tawson and Patrice. Tawson and Patrice laughed as well.

"Aight, man. I'ma get with you…in the mornin'."

"Bye-bye, Capp."

"Goodbye, Patrice."

"You know Kim's been looking for you. I told her you'd been busy studying for your test to get into Law School…" Capp cut her off.

"Graduate School, sweetheart. Grad School. Haven't made it to Law School yet. I will. Just not yet."

Patrice looked at Tawson awkwardly, slapped him on the hand like she was chastising a child, and said, "Tawson, you said Capp was going to Law School."

"No I didn't. I said grad school, girl. You know that."

"No you didn't. You said…"

"Look, come on here. I know what I told you. You just don't be listenin' that's all."

"You two be good tonight, then."

"Aight, man. We're gone. In a minute." Tawson and Patrice both left the hacienda, leaving Capp in complete solitude. He sighed in relief and went to his stash spot to roll himself a blunt of weed.

"Well, back to the grind," he thought. Capp finished rolling the cigar and lit the end. He sat down at the dining room table and reached towards his book bag on the floor. He started to shuffle through it, then paused. He got up from the table, went over to the couch, picked up the remote control, fondled it for a moment, then returned to the dining room table to study for his exam.

"First things first," he said. "I've already played around enough today."

Part 2

The day before Capp was to take the GRE, he decided to stay home and relax. After "shootin' the shit," with Tawson, laughing and joking and smoking massive amounts of weed, Capp decided to lie down and take a nap. Within moments of drifting off, there was a knock on his bedroom door.

"I'ma get out of here a lil' early, man. I left the cable bill on the kitchen counter."

Capp offered no response.

"Nigga, you hear me?"

"Yeah. I hear you…but I'm sleep," Capp groaned through the bedroom door.

"Aight then," replied Tawson.

"Yeah."

After Capp awakened from his doped-up slumber, he decided to scroll through the contacts in his cellular phone to find some company for the evening. He glanced at the clock and noticed it was after ten, and if Tawson wasn't home that meant that he was working and that Capp had the place all to himself. He decided to scroll through his cellular phone to find some company for the night. He was bored with his day of leisure and relaxation and wanted some female companionship. He was feeling "frisky," as he would often say whenever he was sexually aroused, or breathing for that matter. Capp had a penchant for women of all kinds, Black, white, and especially mixed. So much so, that he called himself the 'Mulatto King' because of the number of mixed women, be they Black and white, or white and Mexican, or Mexican and Black, that he had bedded. On this night, none of the women he called had any time to deal with Capp. His only lead came from one of his sexual favorites and nightcap faithfuls, Cleo. It had been a while since Capp had dealt with Cleo, three months to be exact, so his conversation was extremely topical and brief.

"Hello?"

"What's goin' on wit ya?"

"Well, well, well…long time no hear, Mr.. Man."

"You know who this is?"

"Naw. You know I know who this is. How've you been, Caaapp?"

"Oh, how I love the way you say my name…say my name, say my name, when no one is around you, say 'Baby, I love you.'"

"You crazy. Whassup?"

"You, shid."

"Really? Haven't heard from you."

"You know how it is. I been tryin' to get ready for grad school and all."

"You been busy, huh?"

"Yeah. What about you? What you been up to? Tell me somethin' good"

"Nothing much. School. That's about it."

"What you got goin' for tonight?"

"What I got goin for tonight?"

"Yeah, what you got goin' for tonight?"

"Nothin'." (awckward silence)

"You feel like comin' through? Watch a couple of movies?"

"Watch a couple of movieeees?"

"Yeah."

"A couple of movies is gonna be at least three and a half, four hours."

"Yeah."

"Tawson at home?"

"Nope."

"What're you doin'?"

"Nothin'. Watin' on you."

"I'm on my way."

"Cool."

And the deal was sealed. About an hour later, Cleo arrived. Instead of inviting her in, Capp stopped her at the door.

"What it is? You wanna go get a couple of drinks?"

"Uh, sure. Yeah. I don't mind."

"Good. Come in for a sec. Lemme get some cash and then… we can ease on down." Capp went to his bedroom drawer and got some cash and the two were off to the local bar and grill.

After a couple of hours of appetizers and cocktails and conversation that consisted of kinky talk and cock tales, the two decided to return to the apartment. Before they got out of the car, Cleo grabbed Capp's arm as he was trying to open the car door.

"Hold up a second, Capp. I need to talk to you 'bout somethin'."

"Bout what?" That tip I left?" Capp said with a laugh. "I told you I didn't mind payin'. That's the least I could do. I needed this night out. I think I'm ready for that G-R-E now."

"No, Capp. I need to talk to you about somethin' serious."

"Well, let's go upstairs and chit-chat, lil mama. We don't wanna look like we on a stake-out or nothin'."

"No, for real. I need to know if you know a Kim?"

"Do I know a Kim? I know a lot of Kims, Cleo. What you mean?"

"Look, I've been hearin' some things on the yard."

"You been hearin' some things on the yard? I don't even be on campus like that no more. So, you shouldn't be hearin' shit 'bout me." Capp's tone grew demonstrative and heavy.

"Look, I don't care what you do with no other hoes, Capp. Damned me and you. We don't even get down like that no more, so it really don't matter. I know you do your thing. Shit, I got a dude right now and I'm sittin' here drunk with you right now. So, don't start actin' like that."

"Kim, who, Cleo? Kim who?"

"All I know is it is a Kim who be with some chic named Patrice. She got long hair, light-skinned, and skinny. Kinda look like she could model."

"Patrice?"

"Yeah. Patrice."

"Uh…"

"She mess with Tawson, don't she?"

"I don't really know…"

"Ok. Play stupid, Capp. She described ya'll's place to the't'. She said she introduced *Kim* to Tawson's roommate. And ain't you Tawson's roommate?"

"It's...'to the teeth.'"

"What?"

"To the teeth. That's the saying. Like when people say somebody was 'dressed to the teeth,' they mean they were sharp from head to toe, even to their teeth. A lot of people don't know that," Capp paused, voice quivering with nervousness and continued, "It's 'to the teeth.'"

"You know, you're a real smart ass, Capp. Sorry I ain't as well-read as you or in "grad school" like you. But you need to get serious. Cause *this* is serious."

"I *am* serious," Capp replied.

"Look, I don't know how to say this but...that Kim ain't no Kim."

"What you mean? Whatcha talkin' 'bout?"

"Capp."

"Cleo?"

"Look..."

"Look, what? Go 'head and tell me what you tryin' to tell me. Kim who?"

"Kim is John."

"What?"

"Kim is *John*."

"What? John? *John*? What the fu-..."

"Kim is a dude. Kim is a dude, Capp. Kim is a dude named John. That's what I've been tryin' to tell you."

"I don't...I don't believe this shit," Capp stated as his emotions roller-coastered from anger to confusion to bewilderment to anger to despair to self-loathing to confusion to anger again.

"Capp?"

"Yeah. Gimme a minute."

"I didn't want to be the one to tell you this, but..."

"Well, I guess I didn't know *Kim*, did I?"

Cleo frowned with sadness and said, "Capp, you want me to leave?"

"Want you to leave? Why for?'

"Why for? That's cute. You okay?"

"I guess?"

"You didn't do nothin' with dude, did you? Cause I heard he been goin' around dressin' up like a chic and goin' down on some of every dude on the yard. Greeks, athletes, whoever." Capp said not a mumbling word.

"Should I go?"

"No, you shalln't," Capp said with a laugh and a smile. "Dude-thing just got my number that's all. I didn't do shit with *it*."

"Dude-thang. That's what we gone call him, Capp." Cleo began laughing profusely and rocking back in forth in the car seat, patting her knees with the palms of her hands. "Whew, Capp. That's funny. I'm glad you said you didn't let Dude-thang touch you because I've heard some horror stories, girl, oh, I'm sorry, Capp. I done heard some horror stories about what's happened to him for messing with dudes and shit."

"For real? Like what?" Capp replied, fidgeting in his seat.

"Like I heard that Patrice girl be settin' Kim…I mean John… up with the friends of the niggas she be fuckin'. That's so foul, ain't it? And some of them dudes be kissin' on him and lettin' him go down on them and shit."

"Niggas been gettin' head from dude? Aw, shit. Shit, naw!"

"Capp, I ain't seen the John nigga, but do he look like a chic?"

"Naw. Hell, naw. I was fooled. Plus, I really didn't pay much attention to *it*. When Patrice brought Dude-Thing with her to our crib, they only stayed a half hour or so."

"Well, that's good for you. 'Cause baby, I heard she'll suck a dick at the drop of a dime! Real quick, Capp. Real quick," Cleo said, jerking her neck. "Word is he got jumped on a couple of times by some guys who found out Kim was John, you know?"

"Uh, huh," Capp said as he began opening the car door. "You wanna get out of this car and go inside for a little bit. I'm tired of talkin' 'bout cost-cutter Rupaul. I'ma let Tawson know what kinda motherfuckers that Patrice is runnin' with. I don't think I want her at our crib no more."

"Yeah. That's fine. You know, we still got those movies to watch." As Cleo was getting out of the car, Capp swiftly jogged over to the passenger side to assist her.

"Thank you."

"Naw, thank you, Cleo. Good lookin' out. Gotta keep that type of element out of my crib, you dig? Shid, out my life, you feel me?"

"Yep," Cleo replied with a slight smile, sensing that Capp wasn't telling the truth about the extent of his relationship with John because of his uneasiness during the entire revelation. The two went inside and watched a movie, among other things.

The following morning, after Capp saw Cleo to her car, instead of going back to bed, he decided to have a word with Tawson. It was around 6 a.m., so he knew it would be difficult to wake Tawson because of him just getting off of work a couple of hours earlier. After several seconds of knocking and calling his name, Tawson responded with a holler from his bedroom.

"Yeah. Uh-huh!!"

"Taw, man, I need to holla at you for a minute 'bout somethin'."

"Now."

"Yeah. Now."

A few moments later, Tawson came into the living room, shocked to see a visibly disgusted and worried Capp. Still groggy from sleep, Tawson sat on the loveseat next to the sofa where Capp was seated.

"So, wassup? I heard you and *somebody* last night."

"Yeah, fuck all that though.," Capp said, as he paused for a moment then continued, "Taw, man, that Patrice bitch can't come by her no more."

"What?!"

"Yeah, that bitch is bad news, you hear me?"

"Whatcha talkin' about, Capp. Whatcha mean bad news?"

"Last night me and Cleo got together and she told me that Kim is a dude!" Capp grew angry again, much more flustered than the night before when he had first received this revelation.

"Say what!!" Tawson exclaimed loudly.

"Yeah, goddamnit. The Kim bitch is a dude with a dick. Probably bigger than mine and yours put together. No wonder why it didn't wanna do nothin' but suck dicks all night."

"Aw, hell naw! Shit!"

"That's the same shit I said when I heard this shit last night!"

"How do you know Cleo is tellin' the truth about all this?" This shit seems like somethin' from a book or T.V. or somethin'."

"Well, this ain't no fuckin' story or no T.V. show, Taw. This real life. And I'ma get John *and* that Patrice bitch!"

"John?"

"Yeah. That's the nigga's real name. John. A dude named John. Out here dressin' up like a female to fuck with niggas and shit. This shit is ridiculous. I can't believe it either. Plus, Cleo told me that the nigga done done this to plenty of other niggas on the yard. And only God knows who else."

"We need to talk to the other niggas who he done done like this then."

"Shit naw we don't!" Capp exclaimed. "We don't need to tell nobody about this. Nobody. Shid, them motherfuckers handled they shit. And I'ma handle mine too."

"What'd they do?"

"Jumped on the faggot. What you think they did? Cleo told me that much. And I believe it."

"We need to make sure, Capp."

"I been callin' the number all morning and when he finally answered, I said, 'Wassup, John?' and the bitch-nigga hung up the phone."

"What?! Hung up the phone?"

"'Immediately. Soon as I said the motherfucker's name, he hung up. That's how I know this shit is the truth."

"Man, lemme call Patrice and see what the fuck this is all about."

"You ain't gotta see. It's all fallin' in line now. Shid, suckin' dick all night long, swallowing nigggas' nut. Them big ass hands, long fingers like a power forward?... It wouldn't let me take it's clothes off. And it got real nervous when I got to undoing her pants."

"Shid, his pants, Capp."

"Hmph. See, this is what I've been thinkin' about since Cleo told me this shit. A nigga done tricked me to think he's a she, so he can suck my dick. I'm not goin'. Not goin' at all. Period. Shouldn't this be a crime or somethin'?"

"Hell, yeah, it should. But what the police gonna do?"

"You mean to tell me it ain't no crime to impersonate another person?"

"I don't know. Really don't know, Capp. I think it's legal to be a transvestite."

"It shouldn't be," Capp replied sternly, "but I think you need to call Patrice. Cause I need to find out where that nigga John stay."

"Aight. Capp, man, this is really, really fucked up, you know that don't it."

"Do I?" Capp replied.

Part 3

The call to Patrice confirmed the news that Kim was indeed a male named John. After Tawson finished the phone call with Patrice, Capp began plotting his revenge.

"So what'd the Patrice bitch say, Taw?"

"She told me all about the John nigga. She said that the she know the dude from her modeling group or whatever. "

"Modeling group?"

"Yeah."

"Oh, so the motherfucker is a model?! I really don't believe this shit now. So what does the nigga model? Men or women's apparel?"

"I didn't ask all that, Capp," Tawson said with a laugh.

"This ain't funny, nigga. That motherfucker not only violated me, but you too. Don't forget that.   A dude done sucked your dick too, Taw." Momentarily, the conversation ceased.

"You find out where he stay?"

"Don't you got a test to take this mornin'?"

"Yeah. But it's gonna be kinda hard to take it now that this shit done popped off. How a nigga gone concentrate for three or four hours with this hangin' over my head, huh?"

"Since you've already paid for it, I think you should go ahead and take it. We can deal with this shit later."

"Later?"

"Yeah, that dude ain't goin' nowhere. I'll try and get Patrice to tell me where he lives. We gone handle it, Capp. Don't worry about it. Worry about your test for right now."

"You right. I'm gonna get ready. I'ma touch basis with you when I get done."

"Cool."

"Taw, man, we can't let nobody find out about this, you hear me?"

"Yeah, I hear you," Tawson replied forlornly, now feeling the eeriness and confusion that Capp had grappled with all night long, even while he was inside of Cleo.

The isness of the situation had now sunk in completely. The two young men had been sexually manipulated and violated. The games of lust, seduction, and manipulation that they had played with various young women were now the very games that authored the current precarious situation that the two now found themselves in. The cloak of homosexuality now draped over the two young men. They were now ignorant of their own sexuality and feared the psychological consequences of being 'turned out' by a man. This would be their first and only hetero-homosexual encounter.

During the exam, Capp kept thinking of how he had "been" with a man. Maybe he hadn't had intercourse with a man, but he had kissed a man and allowed that man to put his penis in his mouth. He kept wondering how he hadn't noticed that Kim was John. He kept thinking that he should've been aware of the abnormalities that *it* possessed. The short curly hairstyle like a man's. The overly sized hands that were larger than his own. And especially, the insatiable sexual appetite. He kept thinking how it seemed that ' Dude-Thing' was more excited about giving head than he and Tawson were about receiving it.

The GRE was to last four hours, but Capp finished in two and a half hours flat because of the constant distraction that had been racking his brain. Was he or was he not gay because of what had happened to him? Capp had always prided himself on being a 'chief bitch-getter,' as he called himself, and now it seemed as if he was the 'bitch' that was 'gotten' by John. After completing the analytical section of the examination, Capp guessed on over half of the quantitative questions. Never an apt pupil of mathematics, Capp figured he'd have a better chance at getting a decent score guessing on the quantitative section than he would if he actually tried to figure out all of the geometric and algebraic questions on the exam. Capp was a Literature major. He was analytical. That's how he thought. He used his common and learned sense to discern and decipher human situations. In essence, Capp was a literary analyst. And he chose to parlay this skill of his into a career in jurisprudence.

Ironically, the current situation at hand was one that, if he was one who was truly analytical, was discernable from the start. Now that the revelation had been revealed, Capp had been in a continual state of mental mutilation. He chastised himself for being fooled by a transsexual. He remembered over and over again how his father had told him when he was in junior high school to beware of men who dressed like women and drugged men in order to sleep with them, or 'bust they booty' and 'give 'em booty babies,' as his father used to say (a footnote to the story of the Birds and the Bees). At fourteen years old, this story seemed like some fantastical fairy tale, yet now, at twenty-two, his father's fairy tale had materialized.

After leaving the university's testing center, Capp decided to stop by the campus apartments and have another chat with Cleo. When he arrived in the parking lot of the campus apartments, he called Cleo from his cellular phone, yet there was no answer. Instead of leaving, he got out of his car and went to the door. After a few knocks, Cleo's roommate, Tangie, answered the door.

"Hey, Capp!" Tangie said, excited to see him.

"Tangie, hi. How're you?"

"Great. And you?"

"I can't call it."

"I ain't seen you over here in a while. Cleo's not home but you're welcome to come on in and chill."

"Well...I guess I can for a bit," Capp said hesitantly.

"Well, come on in, Mr. Capp," Tangie said with a smile, opening the door wider now, giving Capp ample enough room to enter the apartment.

"Have a seat, Capp. You want somethin' to drink?"

"Naw, I'm good."

"To eat?"

"No, I'm fine."

"Yes you are," Tangie replied with a little sass in her voice.

Tangie's response brought a smile to Capp's face and a light-hearted chuckle to his belly.

"Here, Capp," Tangie said, tossing the remote control from the loveseat to the couch where he was sitting. With heads up reflexes, Capp caught the remote.

"Uh-oh, Capp. You should've played baseball. Been a catcher or somethin'."

"Naw, I hit better than I catch."

"You silly," Tangie replied laughing aloud.

Capp began flicking through the channels on the television, seemingly bored with the programming the stations had to offer at the time.

"You know what time Cleo's gonna be back home?"

"Naw. I think she went to work. You gotta go?"

"I ain't in no rush, but I don't wanta wear welcome out. I just needed to holla at her about somethin'."

"You ain't 'wearin'' out your welcome,' Capp. I don't have nothin' to do. I don't mind your company. Is it anything I can help you with?"

"Naw. It's somethin' that I just needed to ask her."

"Okay."

"Anyways. How's everything with you? School goin' alright?"

"Yep. Pushed that G.P.A. up above a 3.0 this term."

"That's good. Real good, Tangie."

"My folks told me that if I brought my grades up they'd pay for the modeling troop I wanna join."

"Modeling?"

"Yeah. Cleo's the one who put me on to it."

"Cleo?" Capp said with a look of amazement on his face. "I didn't know she was modeling now. She's modeling? Where?"

"They meet and practice for shows at this church. I really don't know where. I ain't from here, so I ain't familiar with the street name or the name of the church. But I do know that it's not far from where you live?"

"How you know?"

"Cleo said it when we were driving there one time. She was just sayin', ,'Capp doesn't live too far from here.'"

"For real?"

"Yeah. Actually, a few of the girls on the yard model with the group."

"How many times have you went with Cleo to a practice or whatever?"

"Quite a few times. Last week we didn't go because she and one of the models…a girl named Patrice, well, I think that's the girl's name, got into it."

"Patrice?"

"Yeah. I didn't know what it was all about until we left. After we got in the car, she said that the Patrice chic had said somethin' about sleepin' with her guy or whatever."

"Who? Cleo's boyfriend?"

"Yeah. I don't know why Cleo was so mad because she does cheat on him anyway, so she shouldn't care if he does the same. Plus, I told her about tellin' all her

personal business to people that she don't really know that well. Especially Patrice. I don't know her, but I've seen her slippin' in and outta plenty different dudes' apartments over here late at night. She got a bad rep."

"Mmph. Looks like ya'll got a soap opera goin' on."

"Naw, Capp," Tangie said laughing again, "That's just Cleo's mess. You know how she can get. She wants all the dudes to herself, you know? She want her cake and eat it too."

"Yeah, me too. Who don't?"

"I heard that. I told Cleo she can't have *all* the men to herself. She gotta share some."

"What'd you say, Tangie? She got learn to share a lil' bit?"

"Yeah. You know? Like with you. A few weeks back, I saw you on campus and told Cleo that I saw you and said that you was lookin' cute. She got all mad about that. Then she asked who you were with and I told her you were walkin' with some girl. Then she asked what the girl looked like and I told her she was a nice lookin' girl. Then she gon' have the nerve to say, 'I bet the bitch don't look better than me.'"

"No she didn't, did she?" Capp replied.

"Yes, she did, Capp. Yes she did. I mean, you could see the jealousy in her face. And I was like, 'Capp ain't your man, girl.' She act like ya'll go together or somethin'. What did you put on her, Capp?"

"I dunno."

"Give me some of that then if it's like that," Tangie said laughingly with a flirtatious smirk on her face. Aroused by the comment, Capp got up from the couch and moved towards the apartment's exit.

"You can have it. But you might not live to tell about it if Cleo finds out. Since you say she so jealous."

"Go 'head, boy," Tangie replied rubbing the side of her thigh with her hand. Clad in black gym shorts, a snug-fitting camouflage tank top, no socks and a pair of beat up New Balance, Tangie's appearance appealed to the mentally beleaguered Capp. He was tired of the mystery that surrounded the 'Dude Thing,' and the perpetrators of the masquerade, Patrice, and now it seemed Cleo as well, were aware of the transsexual's true intentions to deceive and 'turn out' any willing male participants. More and more turned on by Tangie and her flirtatious comments, Capp decided to not only test the waters, but swim in them as well.

"So…you say you don't know when Cleo is gonna come back, huh?" Capp said as he slithered closer to Tangie. She stood at the kitchen entrance, which wasn't far from the apartment door. Capp grabbed her hand and pulled her into the entry hallway with him.

"You wanna know what got Cleo actin' that way, Tangie?"

"Oooh, maybe. But not here. Not now."

Capp pulled Tangie tight to him, pressing his midsection against her own. Feeling his concrete erection, Tangie smiled in amusement.

"Oh-my-God," she said, then whispered with apprehension, "this is bad, Capp.

This is soooo bad." Then, within a blink of an eye, Capp dropped to his knees in worship. He began licking her thighs while grabbing at her breasts like a child reaching for toys.

"Mmph, mmph," she moaned in pleasure.

Capp pulled her gym shorts down to her ankles to subdue her and then went to town on her private place. He stiffened his tongue like an erect penis and plunged it in and out or her vaginal opening, simulating intercourse. Every now and then he'd look up from her womb and see Tangie mumbling inaudible words to herself, saliva running from her mouth with her eyes closed as if hypnotized. When Capp wasn't looking at her, Tangie would look down to see nothing but the top of his head twisting and turning and lunging in between her thighs like a starved-out dingo dog. All the while he was dining on Tangie, Capp was unbuckling his jeans, lifting each leg out of the denims one at a time, and unleashing his penis. Exposed, he began masturbating, hard and fast. After he obtained a rock-hard erection, he helped Tangie get her legs out of the gym-short shackles, turned her around and pinned her up against the wall, as if she was under arrest, and slid his swollen penis inside of her already watery-womb.

He hunched her from behind for a couple of minutes, then turned her around, wrapped one of her legs around his waist and mashed himself inside of her, pumping deep and fast and to the left and to the right. Long strokes. Short, choppy strokes. Hitting her cavern walls, or 'bendin' corners' as he called it, when recanting conquests with the fellas. All the while, Capp would suck and tug on her nipples, attempting to feed on them like an infant.

"Capp, we gotta stop."

"Uh, uh. No we don't."

"Yes we do, Capp. Uh, uh. Just not here…this is soooo bad."

"Ok, then," Capp replied, still inside of Tangie, but no longer pumping as profusely.

"Ok. Good. Whew," Tangie responded.

A few moments went by and neither one of the two moved to kill the beast with two backs. So Capp, hardening and seeming to extend in length a bit, continued his vaginal assault on Tangie. He started licking the fingers on her hands while pounding away at her pelvic area with his pulsating unit. Somewhat upset because of Tangie's refusal to respond when he'd ask, 'You feel that dick?,' Capp grew sexually flustered, as men often due when they feel as if they aren't satisfying their partner. The more he'd ask, the more she'd *not* respond, which in turn caused his anger and pumping to increase. Undoubtedly enjoying the ferocity with which Capp 'threw that dick' as she'd later tell him, Tangie controlled their sexual encounter by dictating the speed, the movement, and the intensity, all by subliminally controlling Capp's thoughts with her nonverbal communication. He thought that if she didn't respond to him, or if Tangie didn't make a lot of unwanted noise during sex, then he wasn't performing well. When in fact, she loved every minute of the time they spent together.

"Ooh, I'ma cum."

"Where?"

"Where you want?"

"Where you want?" Tangie replied.

After hearing this, Capp's erection stiffened. He exited her vaginal area and laid her on her stomach. Rubbing his penis, Capp began licking down Tangie's spine

until he came to the tattoo that sat at the small of her back.

"Nice tat," he whispered.

"Yeah."

"Whose names are these?"

"The name on the rose is my great-grandmamma and grandmamma, they both died a few years back, and the names on the vines are my mamma, and my three sisters," Tangie whispered.

"That's real," Capp replied, not necessarily moved by the sentimental reasoning behind Tangie's ink fetish. Now, he started to lick the rose and the vines and the names that were tattooed on her backside. He spread her buttocks and began licking and sucking her vaginal lips. He once again inserted himself inside of her. Grinding and jerking inside of her like a madman, Capp pulled his penis from inside of Tangie and came all over the deceased. He continually jerked, pumped, and drained his penis until no more semen spewed from the head.

"Yes sir!" Capp exclaimed, sitting on the back of Tangie's thighs.

"Get up, boy," Tangie said with a laugh. "You ain't light, ya know?"

"Shid, you know I can swallow a strand of spaghetti and be full. Play hide-and-go-seek behind an ink pen and win," Capp said jokingly, now putting all of his weight on the back of her thighs.

"Get up, shit!" Tangie blurted out, growing a tad frustrated with Capp's antics. He obliged her demands and swiftly began dressing.

"Can I use your bathroom for a minute?"

"Yeah. Lemme get you a couple of towels."

"A couple? I'm a dude. I only got one hole to wash."

"Capp…you are so nasty. I'ma get you two anyway. Wash and dry, baby. Wash and dry."

Part 4

As Capp was leaving the campus apartments, he saw Cleo driving into the entrance. Instead of blowing his horn, he shied away from her, tilting his head to the right, away from the steering wheel, as to not come into eye contact with her. This allowed his exit to be an inconspicuous one. When he arrived home, Tawson was in the living room on the telephone. He placed his index finger against his lips, motioning to Capp to keep quiet and mouthing the words, 'This Patrice.' After a couple of minutes, the phone call was terminated.

"So, what'd the bitch say," Capp said with contempt.

"She confirmed the shit, man," Tawson replied. The room grew uneasily silent with Tawson's reply.

"Hmm?"

"How'd your test go?" Tawson said, trying to avoid the obvious tension that hovered above the both of them.

"Man…I can't call it. I pretty much guessed on the quantitative shit. Fuck all them mathematical equations and scenarios and what not…It just wasn't my day today. I think I did pretty good on all of the analytical questions and the analogies, but the quantitative portion kicked-my-assets, you hear me?"

"I hear you, man," Tawson replied with a laugh.

"But anyway…"

"Yeah, man, Patrice told me the business. They got a rehearsal at that church down the street. She said it was at the corner of Gemini and Beaverwood. We can stop by their if you wanna catch dude and holla at him. Cause to tell you the truth, I been thinkin' 'bout this shit since you told me this mornin' and it ain't sittin' well with me either, man. No bullshit."

"Square biz then. What time did she say they were gon' be there?"

"Seven. Rehearsal lasts about two or three hours."

"Yeah. Well, we gon' post up outside of *rehearsal* until that nigga come out, Taw! See how much he like dick then."

Around six in the evening, Capp and Tawson began rolling blunt after blunt, continuously reliving the incident in which John 'turned them out.' The more they recanted the events, the more the two, young men endured the humiliation that they had never known until the revealing of Kim's true identity. Capp kept wondering to himself, *'Did Cleo tell me the truth about Kim because she's trying to help me...or is she just trying to get back at Patrice in some warped way of thinking because she fucked her boyfriend? Because if I hadn't have stopped by and talked to Tangie, I might've not known what her intentions really were. This is fucked up. These bitches done ran plenty of game on us. Fuck us! Me, goddamnit!! I just should've known somethin' was up with that Kim...or John...goddamned. A female ain't just gone wanna suck on a hard ass dick without puttin' it between her legs. I know if I'ma eat some pussy, I'ma wanna put my dick in it too. Damned, I'm a stupid ass nigga. Fuck, Fuck, Fuck, Fuck, Fuck!! I should've known. I should've known, goddamnit.'*

Seven thirty rolled around and Capp and Tawson were still smoking.

"You ready to ride, Taw?"

"When you are," Tawson said with a shrug and a sigh.

"Let's vamp then," Capp said and the two departed their place of residence.

After locating the church at the corner of Gemini and Beaverwood, they reached the church where Patrice said the rehearsal was to be held. They entered the church parking lot and parked on the side of the building where the truck was out of view, yet the two could peer into the window of the room in the church where the 'models' were rehearsing. Tawson chose to drive, so he had total control of the wheel.

"What you wanna do, Capp, man?"

"Post up."

"Post up? We might as well gone on in there and confront dude."

"Naw, naw. We don't wanna cause no uproar. We just gon' sit back, wait on them to get finished. Catch the nigga on his way to the car…."

"Mmm, hmm, Okay. I got ya. You think the nigga gon' fight back? Or call the police or some shit like that?"

"Call the po-lice? How a nigga gone call the po-lice and tell 'em,'Officer, two niggas jumped on me cause I sucked they dick when I was Halloweenin' as a female?' That shit sound so crazy! Don't worry about what that nigga gon' do. Just know that I'ma whip that motherfucker's ass. This one dick he gone wish he never sucked, you hear me?"

"Yeah, yeah. Fuck that though, Capp. There they go there," Tawson said, abruptly turning the key in the ignition.

Patrice, two tall, long, slender women, and John disguised as Kim were going to their car while laughing with a few other young, attractive, well-dressed women with duffle bags and handfuls of clothing. After the group of women dispersed, going to their respective cars, and presumably home, Patrice and John got into another car parked directly in front of the building. Patrice got into the back seat while John rode shotgun. Capp and Tawson ceased the waylay.

"Is that a nigga or a bitch drivin' that car?"

"Don't know, Taw. But whoever it is need to keep betta company, you hear me? Ride up on that motherfucker, man," Capp bellowed with a contemptuous scowl written all over his face.

"Aight," Tawson replied.

"Don't fuck 'em in the ass. Hang back a bit, man."

"Yeah."

Once the car exited the parking lot, Capp grew more anxious. He was fidgeting in the passenger seat and his hands and voice began to tremble as if in fear.

"Let that motherfucker get to the light. Then I'ma jump out the truck, try and pull the nigga out of the car and squirrel his ass."

" I'm gone stop the truck and get out to make sure the driver don't jump in it."

"They can jump in if they want."

"I hear you."

"Speed up a little, man. If they go through that light, we gon' have to run it too."

"Aight."

Tawson shifted the gears on the truck, sped up, and began the hot pursuit. The

black Chevy S-10 loped through the red light, swiftly gaining on the vehicle. The two automobiles came upon another stop light, this one turning red as well. This time the car being hunted adhered to the rules of the road. When the car idled at the stoplight, Tawson kissed the butt of the car with the nose of his Chevy. Capp pressed the button on his seatbelt, jumped out of the passenger side of the truck, and ran up to the car, yanking John from the front seat.

"Whassup, John?" Capp said, yanking him by his blouse. "Nigga, get your ass out that motherfuckin' car!"

By this time, Tawson had gotten out of the truck to make sure no one jumped in to help John. Patrice sat silently in the backseat of the car while the driver, a female, began cursing and yelling at Capp.

"What the fuck are you doing? Stop it! Let go of her!" she said.

"Her? Her? Bitch, this a nigga with a dick 'tween his legs, goddamnit! Stay outta my shit and mind your own fuckin' business," Capp said, still tussling with John.

"Get your hands off me, nigga!" John declared with a voice deep like a man. Capp released him and backed back a few paces.

"Aw, you ain't even gone disguise your voice now, huh, dude?"

John said not a mumbling word. In fact, neither Tawson, Patrice, Capp, nor the female driver said a mumbling word. Then, after a few seconds of disturbing silence, Capp flew into John with a barrage of right and left fists of fury to the face. With malice and rage scrawled across his face, Capp began to mock John.

"Fight back, faggot! Fight back!"

"Get in the Car, Kim! Get in the car," Patrice and the driver screamed.

During the melee , the stoplight had changed from red to green five or six times.

"Whip that motherfucker, Capp!" Tawson yelled.

Hearing this angered John and he began battling back. In fact, he began getting the better of Capp. John, when looked upon as a woman was just considered a beautiful, Amazon because of *her* height and stature, but as a man, he was taller than Capp, and probably outweighed the slender Capp by twenty or twenty-five pounds. After seeing him take a kick to the stomach and four, punishing haymakers to the right side of his head, Tawson jumped into the skirmish.

"Get off my nigga, bitch-ass motherfucker!" Tawson threw two quick jabs to the nose and mouth of John, while Capp was shaking off the daze from the haymakers, and that was all. John screamed in anger and kicked Tawson in the groin.

"I got ya bitch, nigga." By this time, Capp had recovered and resumed pummeling John with too many punches and knees to the stomach to count.

"Stop! Stop!" The girls continued to scream at Capp. "He done had enough. Leave him alone, damned!!" With all of his might, John managed to grab Capp by the waist, pick him up, and dump him on the ground with amazing force and ferocity. Landing on his wrists, Capp lay on the ground clutching himself in pain. This allowed John the time to quickly scamper back into the car, bumbling and stumbling into the vehicle, barely escaping further attack. As the car sped off through the light, Capp yelled, "Fuck you, bitch-ass boy!" while he helped Tawson up from the pavement.

"That nigga kicked me in the nuts, man, damned. Shit my nuts!"

"Yeah, I saw that, Taw. I saw that. That was some dirty shit. But I bet that motherfucker finna go home and lick them goddamned wounds."

"He probably on his way to the emergency room, man. Capp, man you really got in that nigga's shit. You were really fuckin' him up, man. I'm kinda glad that motherfucker got away. We coulda really hurt dude."

"Hell, he coulda hurt us, dude," Capp responded sharply.

"And them girls wuhn't helpin' a bit. We lucky nobody called the police."

"As we know of. Taw, man, we need to get the fuck on down."

"Aight, man. But I'ma have to stop at a gas station and get some ice or some shit. Man, I think I got blue balls.," Tawson said, still gasping and panting for air. The two got into the truck and 'got the fuck on down.' Unable to drive, Tawson pulled over a few blocks away from the incident, and Capp drove the rest of the way home, stopping for a bag of ice at the gas station as suggested.

The next day, neither Capp nor Tawson spoke of the incident. Still sore from the scuffle, Capp took the next couple of days off from work to recuperate. A few days went by and still neither of the young men spoke much of the incident. A few times Capp asked Tawson had he heard from Patrice, and the answer was always the same, "Naw, she ain't called, man." After two weeks with no word from Patrice, Tawson and Capp both came down with the same peculiar symptoms, a pain in the scrotum and bloody urine. Both young men initially kept this knowledge to themselves, but after a few days of uncomfortable urination, they confided in each other one evening while they were watching television.

"Look man, I believe that Patrice bitch done gave me somethin'."

"Like what, Taw? What you mean? Cause whatever she gave you, I might have too. You know, I went into that thang raw too," Capp said cautiously.

"Man, I been seeing blood in my pee and…"

"Me too," Capp replied, interrupting Tawson.

"Man, this is too much."

"Shit. You been to the clinic yet?"

"Nope."

"You?"

"Naw," Capp snapped.

"I think I'ma go down to the free clinic today and see what the fuck is up."

"Yeah. I'ma go to the doctor myself. We know we ain't supposed to be pissin' blood." Capp released a heavy sigh. "I'm gonna go to my folks' doctor. Somebody I know. I can't go down to the free clinic. I've heard war stories about that place. You probably gone be down there all day long, around the dirtiest, filthiest, poorest, most vagrant niggas in town. And they say the nurses down there tell all of your business. They be hollerin' out what they found wrong with you and shit. Naw, I can't do it."

Tawson laughed and replied, " Vagrants? I thought you were done studying for the vocabulary on the GRE. You act like I'm goin' to Hell."

"Might as well be, damned."

"I'm tryin' to find out what's wrong with me. I'm goin' to the doctor, not the club," Tawson said with sarcasm.

"Still, I'm just sayin'..."

"But it's free though," Tawson responded. The next day, they each went for their respective visits. Capp paid and Tawson went for free. Later that evening, Tawson came home and told Capp about his visit to the clinic. Capp listened yet was disgusted because he was unable to see his doctor because of an overbooking of appointments.

"Well, Taw. What'd they say down there?"

"They gonna have my results back in a week."

"What about you?"

"I didn't get to see my doctor, man. They overscheduled their appointments for the day."

"Told you to go down to the free clinic. Wasn't nobody down there today. It was maybe three..four people in front of me. I had to be down there for no more than an hour."

"Word?"

"Yeah, man. Show your ID, sign in, and wait for the nurse to call you back. She gone stick a real thin pin in your dick head and that's that on that."

"Say what? A pin in my dick head?"

"Not in your dick head. In your pee hole."

"My pee hole? Damned, man, that's even worse."

"It's just a pin with a cotton schwab on the end of it, that's all, man. Trust me. It ain't that bad."

"I guess not. I'ma go down there tomorrow morning."

"Yeah. Go 'head and take care of that. The sooner we know what's up, the better off we'll be."

"That's right. That's right," Capp replied. "I'ma be down there first thing in the mornin'."

A week later, Capp and Tawson called the clinic and received their test results. Both of their results were the same. They were tested for Syphilis, Gonorrhea, and Chlamydia. The attendant on the line told both Capp and Tawson the same thing,

"Negative for Syphilis, negative for Gonorrhea, and positive for Chlamydia."

Afterwards, the two of them revealed the outcome of their results. After a few moments of silence and awkward looks at one another, the two shook their heads and, simultaneously said, "That's what we get." The two men laughed an uncomfortable laugh.

"At least this shit can be cleared up, man. That's the good thing."

"Yeah, man. You're right," Tawson said, still shaking his head in disbelief.

"The nurse told me to come back down there and get the prescription for the medicine and to let her know the names of the people I've had sexual contact with in the last six months."

" Me too. Me too. Man, you gone tell 'em 'bout…"

"Hell naw!" Capp interjected. "If the nigga got the clap, oh well. Shid the only way he'd have gotten it from us is if he swallowed it, you hear me? Fuck dude. I couldn't care less what he know or what he got."

"I guess we kinda got out good, man. I mean, ain't no tellin' how many dudes the John nigga and Patrice done done like this."

"Let hit raw and everything."

"Yeah."

"Who knows, man? Who knows? I guess it's like my daddy says, 'Gotta be careful what and who you put your swipe in.'"

"What your daddy call it, Capp? A swipe?"

"Yeah. Your dick."

"I know. I know," Tawson replied with a smile and a laugh. Now, Capp began to smile and laugh as well. The first real smiles and laughs the two had had together since their run in with John.

As the coming weeks passed, life got back to normal for Capp and Tawson. They worked and they played. Tawson continued school the following semester, and, even though Capp's GRE score was below the minimum allowed for admittance to graduate school, he was admitted because of his solid G.P.A. of 3.5 and was placed on a conditional waiver that allowed him to be partially admitted to the graduate program and fully admitted once he made the minimum score on the Graduate Records Examination (which he would two weeks after the new semester began). Tawson and Capp neither spoke of the physical encounters that they had with Kim-John, or 'Dude Thing', nor heard from or tried to contact Patrice. There remained an unspoken bond between the two for the rest of their lives. They had endured something that most men and women never have to experience on Earth, true self-defining. They each had to come to terms with what had happened, who had done this to them, and why. It wasn't John's fault for dressing up as Kim, nor was it Patrice's fault for bringing a man disguised as a woman to entice heterosexual men to participate in homosexual activities, but it was the young men's insatiable sexual appetite that lured them into the lascivious behavior that led them to Kim.

Several years later, Capp was watching the evening news at home alone, when he saw a story about a seventeen-year-old who had been charged with the murder of a man who he had allegedly been romantically involved with. The anchor reported that the teen was unaware of the sexual identity of the man, who was impersonating a woman, and the teen had confessed that the murder was retaliation for the man's concealing of his identity. Startled and drug back into the past by the nightly news, Capp was taken aback, laughed disturbingly and reached for the telephone. Dialing Tawson's number seemed to take an eternity. He shook his head after the fifth or sixth ring, and placed the telephone onto the charger. There was no need to bring up the past. Besides, he wasn't sure that the murder victim was John or not. The news had released neither a name nor age. He smiled. He was glad Tawson didn't answer. It had been years since they had encountered John and what seemed to be even longer since they had spoken with Kim.

PIPERS
GAP

The screen door to our home flung open, wide as the chasm between heaven and hell, as three black policemen rushed inside searching for a burglar, who had last been seen robbing the neighborhood cleaners. No knock, no 'May we speak with the man of the house,' no nothing. Those monsters bombarded our home with all the tact of an elephant on eggshells. My mother was in the bathroom when the policemen barged into our home. My father, the man of the house, was nowhere to be found. Only my mother, my siblings, and myself were there to endure the wrath of Pipers Gap's finest.

"Where the hell is he?" stated one of the officers, who seemed to be the spokesperson for the other two Neanderthal men of the law who, instead of preferring to speak as humans, found nothing better to do than to taunt and fondle my sisters while my brothers watched in fear and fury.

"Where is who?" I shouted to the tall, slender policeman, whose bottom lip was red like a plum, while his top lip was as black as soot in a fireplace. I distinctly remember his left eye maintaining a twitch while his right eye remained still as if the eye, independent of the rest of his body, had been stricken with paraplegia.

"We lookin' for a white boy who done got himself in some hot agua."

"What are you talking about," I said, frowning with disgust.

With a lightning quick reflex, the policeman grabbed me by the collar and yelled, "The peckerwood who robbed the damned cleaners on McLemore Street."

Before I could give a reply, he turned me loose and trudged his way to the back of the house. His henchmen followed and barged into the bathroom where my mother was preoccupied. As I frantically dashed towards the bathroom, I heard an awful screech followed by distinct laughter. When I saw my mother, bloomers shackled at her ankles like a slave, tears hunting one another en route to the bottom of her face, I felt utterly helpless and subject to the whimsical actions of the local policemen sent to terrorize the "white" area of a town, not much different from any town in America in those days.

BEGINNINGS

My father was absent, apparently out doing his superfluous business about town. Therefore, there was no dominant adult in our presence to protect our family from unjust interrogation. After the policemen had exhausted the possibility of finding the imaginary culprit at the home of eight children and an innocent woman, who had never committed a crime in her life except for surrendering herself to a desolate situation with a man who reeked of negligence, they vacated the premises. We never discussed the incident with my father after he arrived home hours later. This one incident would haunt my mother until her death, not because of the personal humiliation, but because her children had witnessed the humiliation while her husband, *our* father, was absent at a time in which he was desperately needed. This was just one of the many degrading instances that marred the substance of my childhood. I would be viciously raped of my innocence and emotionally molested at the hands of negligence and passion.

Summers were hot in Pipers Gap, yet everyday seemed hotter than the previous scorcher that had inhabited our quaint little town. Pipers Gap was located seventy-five miles outside of Memphis. Close enough for my eyes to wander, yet far enough for my dreams to remain stagnate. Looking back on the distance between my hometown and the bustling bluff city of Memphis, it was really quite minute. But to a poor, white kid from the country, those gravel roads leading to the big city seemed longer than train smoke.

My father, Luther Goins, was a small, thin man of about five feet six inches tall and no more than one hundred forty pounds with full body armor. He possessed dark green eyes and he had paper-thin lips similar to the wicked line that so often poses as a mouth for the run-of-the-mill garden snake. He had a mangy, brown mop for hair that was rarely in tact and no facial hair, somewhat reminiscent of a eunuch. He was born in Sardis, Mississippi and raised in Antioch. At the age of thirty-two, he married my mother, Beale, and they moved to Tennessee in hopes of a better life. My mother was valedictorian of her eighth grade class, a mammoth accomplishment for a white woman in 1938. My father on the other hand was uneducated and relished in his ignorance. He relied on what he called his "wit," which he improperly spelled as he often wrote it on paper, to propel him to a descent existence.

"Boy, the only way for a white man to keep up with the Pipers Gap nigger is to outwit him," my father used to say. Unfortunately, my father was unsuccessful in "outwitting" the Negroes of Pipers Gap.

By the time my parents settled in Tennessee, my father began to physically, socially, and emotionally enslave my mother by orchestrating consecutive pregnancies. In the span of fifteen years, my mother bore nine children. The eldest, Luther Jr., Ernestine, Ruth, Theodore, myself, the unnamed child, who died during labor, Rivers, Victoria, and Ronald, my youngest brother who suffered from chronic diabetes. My mother, having only completed the eighth grade, was a well-rounded individual who had a zest and admiration for the higher arts. Though my father was damned near a caveman when it pertained to social etiquette and the arts, he gave my mother the right to name me. My mother, being a well-read individual, named me Sebastian, after the classical composer Johan Sebastian Bach. This angered my father, but she coaxed him into allowing my surname to remain by obliging him in his request to name any other offspring they would eventually have.

As a child growing up in Pipers Gap, I detested the name. What did a poor kid like myself know or need to know about composers of classical music? All of the boys in my neighborhood teased me profusely and my surname was the cause of many suspensions from school and the barbaric fisticuffs that awaited me in the neighborhood. Girls seemed to like my name. It was a breath of fresh air in the community considering the majority of the words uttered were of negative connotation. "Peckerwood," "Honkey," "Cracker!" The blacks in Pipers Gap seemed to have it out for the white man in general. It wasn't enough that the county was almost completely run by blacks, but they would make an extra effort in attempting to keep whites mentally, socially, and economically in the dark.

My father had numerous odd jobs. All working for black folks. My brothers and I all worked for my father once we were old enough to lift a shovel, broom, or hoe. I didn't mind working for my father when I was a child because it offered me the luxury of being able to see the fruits of success that life had to offer. The homes that black people lived in were extremely elegant, yet somewhat gaudy. One man's home, Mr. Raddoff, resides vividly in my memory because of the numerous amounts of money he had lying around. Mr. Raddoff was a wealthy man and extremely hard to please. I remember my father saying, "Raddoff is a nigger that wants somethin' for nothin' and that's exactly what I'm gonna give him. Nothin' for somethin'."

Mr. Raddoff was about six feet six inches tall and had to have weighed well over two hundred fifty pounds. It was all muscle and it showed through the heavy starch in which he wore in his shirts. His stomach was like a washboard that protruded through his Oxford cloth shirts and his thighs were massive and looked as if he had traded his legs at birth with a Clydesdale. He owned five cars and a fair skinned wife who had physical features similar to that of a white woman. My father rendered services such as lawn care, plumbing, carpentry, and basically whatever one needed to be done around the home. My father, a jack of all trades, yet a master of none.

Mr. Raddoff made his fortune by being born the only namesake to a multi-millionaire. His father, Herbert Raddoff, the family patriarch, gained earthly treasures by selling numerous acres of land in which he owned to white buyers for triple and often times quadruple the value. Mr. Raddoff, whose first name I never knew, once said, "No peckerwood should be allowed to know, let alone speak the first name of a blue-blooded Negro." He inherited the family fortune and the remaining land, which was well over half the land in Pipers Gap. But my father had a way with Negroes and the Negroes that patronized him knew it. Black folks seemed to own the world and it was the white man's occupation or *duty* to make him feel more comfortable. Our recompense was to keep plugging away at that rock and maybe one day it would give way.

I had a front row seat on Mondays, Wednesdays, and Fridays at what Negro life was like because the Raddoffs were the epitome of success in Pipers Gap. The air even seemed fresher in their yard. An exhibitionist of opulence, Mrs. Raddoff never displayed repetition. We worked for them seven years, visited three times a week, twelve months a year, and I never saw her in the same clothes. My brothers and I manicured the yard to perfection while my father either worked inside the house or gallivanted the streets until our tasks were complete for the day.

The Raddoff account paid quite well, so it wasn't a problem for my father to waste an entire day, three days a week, at their home. Plus, Mr. Raddoff enjoyed playing the big shot and marveled at the sight of a yard full of white men slaving away to keep his plantation-like estate appearing as a modern day Garden of Eden. To top it all off, Mr. Raddoff would speak to my father as if he was lower than a snake's dick. He would often quip, "Luther, you and your boys remind me of what I don't wanna be reminded of." Laughter would follow this statement from he and my father. Ironically, Raddoff had no idea that the man he routinely ridiculed, and sympathetically employed, would taint his prized possession, Mrs. Raddoff, beyond social recognition.

NEGLIGENCE

My father had a way with women and knew that there were only two things women couldn't resist, a hot meal and money. Being the philanthropist he was, Luther supplied them with both. My mother knew of these rolls in the grass in which my father participated, yet she remained in the marriage because divorce was unheard of in a solid, Christian home. And white women in Pipers Gap, most of them being either teachers or maids, could not afford a divorce.

My father's exploits were expensive and costly. It showed in his maintenance of our family and home. Our utilities were off more than on thanks to my father apparently believing that electricity was free, and our cupboards were so bare that the rats would boycott and strike. Our entire street knew of my father's negligence. So of course, my siblings and myself involuntarily assumed the role of the neighborhood laughing stocks.

Luther's destructive behavior particularly interrupted my scholastic performance because the lack of financial stability at home led to my inadequate amount of school supplies and clothing. (A hungry child makes for a poor performing pupil) My mother and father argued all night, whenever he decided to retire for the night, which caused me to also suffer from sleep deprivation. I felt as if I was a vampire. Up all night. Asleep all day. The daytime offered me the opportunity to count sheep, but unfortunately that was when the teacher was teaching, and that caused horrific episodes at school.

"God, get me out." I used to pray daily. I couldn't for the life of me figure out why *my* life was so dismal. I was poor. My parents were constantly at odds with one another, and we spent more and more time slaving at the Raddoffs. The worst thing in the world is for one who is ill to continuously be in the company of one who is healthy. An ill individual will become more ill through his envy and need for what the healthy individual possesses. Therefore, the constant trips to the Raddoff home made me sick, in mind and spirit.

My father was not only a con man, he was also a vivacious character that indulged in excess in every aspect of his life. Every man has his vice. My father's was women. Luther lived his life in opposites. He showered his mistresses with gifts, expensive meals, and money, while his wife and children ate sparingly and frequently went without the necessities of life such as electricity and proper seasonal attire. Our wardrobes were about as snazzy as the local hobo. Luther's exploitative ways worked magic with the local poor, white trash women, but would have no effect on his only unconquered conquest, Mrs. Raddoff. He had always fooled around with a black woman here or there, but never with one with as much style, grace, beauty, and especially high societal rank as the angelic Mrs. Raddoff.

ENDINGS

My father always ate two nectarines during our stay at the home of the Raddoffs. One for himself, and one that he would share with that yellow seraphim that occupied the euphoria in which I labored. Mrs. Raddoff seemed to have no respect for her marriage vows in which she had solemnly sworn to many years earlier. This was evident because she sashayed around my father in the way a prostitute would a patron. So lustful her eyes would yearn while Luther, the garden snake, would sit entranced by the gaze of the yellow-black beauty.

I will never forget the day my life changed forever. One suspiciously cool July day, my father and Mrs. Raddoff were in the kitchen, supposedly contemplating the cause of the sudden influx of ants into the Raddoff's personal nirvana. My brothers had been dropped off at another job site, so I toiled alone that particular day.

As I worked in the flower bed located under the kitchen window, I stumbled upon a sight that even now limits my cognitive abilities and sane judgment. Mrs. Raddoff and Luther engulfed in a passionate embrace. Luther's coveralls were shackled at his ankles while Mrs. Raddoff's torso and arms were sprawled on the countertop. Her face buried in a left-handed oven mitt with the muffled yelps of a housewife escaping through the fabric. I stood paralyzed yet my eyes stayed fixed to each animalistic, pelvic thrust in which Luther inflicted upon Mrs. Raddoff. The pit of my stomach burned, my mouth became as dry as the Mojave Desert and my heart stopped and started seven times. On the seventh start, I regained my senses and buried my head in the mulch and red and white begonias. As the tears and mulch formed a ropy residue on my eyelids, I counted to three and rose to my feet to see Mr. Raddoff on top of my father on the kitchen floor, methodically choking the life out of him. With my feet implanted in concrete, I watched as Luther lay on the floor squirming and wriggling for his life as if he was a snake in the mouth of a mongoose.

The fracas caused the police to come and arrest my father for disturbing the peace and attempted rape. Of course, Mr. Raddoff couldn't allow his fellow Negro comrades to find out that a pale face had had his way with his precious, yellow daffodil. So, instead, he told the police, "I found this honkey in my house gropin' my wife, an' he would've had her if I hadn've come home. After all I done for this peckerwood?!" One of the policemen, a short, thin, well groomed, brown skinned Negro with a satin mustache-goatee combination and a curly black mop for hair replied, "I'd forgive him, Mr. Raddoff, for this cracker know not what he do." A perverse guffaw bellowed from the policeman as if he had front row seats to a minstrel show. My father's eyes sunk deep into their sockets as if he heard the cry of a banshee and he slumped into the back of the squad car. I assumed that Luther would be beaten up by the time he was released, if he were ever released any time soon. He never was. My father was found hanging from the ceiling of his cell three days after the arrest. The police said it was suicide, but my mother believed different. Often times white men would be arrested in town and either return home severely beaten, or sometimes not at all. My mother never acknowledged the alleged crime committed by my father, nor the police, but I always did. My siblings were indifferent because none of them truly had a paternal relationship with Luther.

Two weeks later, my mother arranged the funeral. The ceremony was brief, and the turn out was scarce. Exactly seven people besides the immediate family attended the services. The seven outsiders were all my father's allies in his sacred world of capriciousness and infidelity. My mother always said, 'Foolishness follows you to the grave,' and the sight of Luther's court jesting friends looming over his casket further validated her adage. Looking down at the body that was once occupied by a man who was fifty percent responsible for me obtaining life, I smiled half-heartedly. I never felt cheated by having had death strip me of my relationship with my father, because Luther and I never had a *true* relationship. He was just the seed that fertilized the soil that bore me. He was simply a man I once knew.

ABOUT THE AUTHOR

A product of the divisive ra-
cial ideologies of the South,
Gee Joyner was reared in an
upper-class suburban enclave
that allowed him to channel
his distinct, and often times
uncanny perception of American culture, through Man's
first, and most profound me-
dium, the written rhetoric.

Having obtained both
a Bachelors and Masters degree in English Literature
from the University of Memphis, he has utilized his rhetorical
prowess as an empowering tool of social commentary to record
the dichotomy and disturbing behaviors indicative of God's won-
derful and complex creation; humanity.

After surviving an attempted murder in 2002 and using
his skills in composition to aid and assist troubled juveniles in
their quest to overcome the sociopolitical, economical, and
violent pitfalls indicative of U.S. culture, Joyner now embarks on
a sojourner to infiltrate the literary world by documenting *his* take
on America and the attributes thereof that define what it truly is
to be *American*.

His Masters thesis, *White Man's Fame, Black Man's Shame:*
The American Textual Canon's Negative Depiction of African

American's in Mass Media, resides in the Ned McWherter Library at the University of Memphis and is a document of depth that further explains his literary, social, and cultural convictions. An intellect, scholar, and rhetorical genius, Joyner lies in wait as America's next literary laureate.

In the vein of William Shakespeare, William Faulkner, Ralph Ellison, Nella Larsen, James Baldwin, and Toni Morrison, Gee Joyner's works are destined to be blueprints for future writers of substance, and transcendent, and omnipotent content.

-Navar Ero

Printed in the United States
143634LV00002B/10/P

9 781434 348258